Do Princesses Make Happy Campers?

Carmela LaVigna Coyle Illustrated by Mike Gordon

TAYLOR TRADE PUBLISHING

Lanham · New York · Boulder · London

Published by Taylor Trade Publishing
An imprint of The Rowman & Littlefield Publishing Group, Inc.
4501 Forbes Boulevard, Suite 200, Lanham, Maryland 20706
www.rowman.com

Unit A, Whitacre Mews, 26-34 Stannery Street, London SE11 4AB, United Kingdom

Distributed by NATIONAL BOOK NETWORK

British Library Cataloguing in Publication Information Available

Library of Congress Cataloging-in-Publication Data
Coyle, Carmela LaVigna.
Do princesses make happy campers? / by Carmela LaVigna Coyle ;
illustrated by Mike Gordon.
pages cm
ISBN 978-1-63076-054-0 (cloth) — ISBN 978-1-63076-055-7 (electronic)
[1. Stories in rhyme. 2. Camping—Fiction. 3. Family life—Fiction. 4. Princesses—Fiction. 5. Questions and answers—Fiction.] I. Gordon, Mike, 1948 March 16– illustrator.
II. Title.
PZ8.3.C8396Dk 2015
[E]—dc23
2014025477

Manufactured by Midas Printing International
Printed in Huizhou, Guangdong, PRC, China, August 2015

To Annie, Nicky, and Mike,
my compadres in "blue sky and s-u-n."
—c l v c

To my kids, Jay, Kim, Carl, and Lucy,
who taught me the importance of working harder.
—Dad

Do princesses spend hours shopping in stores?

Let's get this family to the great outdoors!

Do princesses help with packing the gear?

Why does it seem like it's taking all year?

Do princesses ask
if we're almost there?

ARE WE THERE YET?

ARE WE THERE YET?

ARE WE THERE YET?

Sometimes they ask with repetitive flair.

Can a princess help you set up the tent?

Perhaps we should make it a family event.

What will we do if it rains all day?

We could stay in the tent and put on a play.

Does a princess make houses
for fairies and gnomes?

Pinecones and twigs will make magical homes!

Pleeeeease can I keep all the critters I find?

Their mommies insist we leave them behind.

I bet you can guess what this princess is wishing . . .

Instead of the dishes she'd rather go fishing?

Do princesses bike
over mountain and brook?

Sometimes they rest at the trail overlook.

Is there always a hush
at the top of the hill?

Mother Nature enjoys being quiet and still.

I'm so hungry I could eat like a bear.

Please try to remember your manners and share.

How come the campfire crackles and roars?

I think it's requesting that we make s'mores!

Why are the stars extra twinkly and bright?

That's how the stars bid a princess "goodnight."

How does the path know the right way to bend?

Because it already knows the way to . . .

THE END.